characters created by
lauren child

I WANT
to be much
more bigger
like you

PUFFIN

Text based on the script written by Carol Noble

Illustrations from the TV animation produced by Tiger Aspe

PUFFIN BOOKS
Published by the Penguin Group: London, New York, Australia,
Canada, India, Ireland, New Zealand and South Africa
Penguin Books Ltd, Registered Offices: 80 Strand, London WC2R 0RL, England

puffinbooks.com

This edition published in Great Britain in Puffin Books 2012
001 – 10 9 8 7 6 5 4 3 2 1
Text and illustrations copyright © Lauren Child/Tiger Aspect Productions Limited, 2008
Charlie and Lola word and logo ® and © Lauren Child, 2005
Charlie and Lola is produced by Tiger Aspect Productions
All rights reserved
The moral right of the author/illustrator has been asserted
Manufactured in China
ISBN: 978-0-718-19524-3
This edition produced for the Book People Ltd,
Hall Wood Avenue, Haydock, St Helens, WA11 9UL

I have this little sister Lola.
She is small and very funny.
        Lola says, "I'm not small, Charlie.
I am getting more **bigger**
        and grown-up all of the time."

"And now that I am
much more **bigger**,
I can go on the
Super-Duper Loopy Loopy ride."

"Aaaagghh!"

So I say,
"The Super-Duper
Loop the Looper is very, **very SCARY**.
Are you sure?"

"I am **very** sure, Charlie," says Lola.

So I measure Lola to see
if she really is **bigger**.

"Charlie, I must be more **taller** than that!
Are you **tricking** me?"

"No, Lola. That's exactly how **big** you are."

Then Lola says,
"But I absolutely MUST be
big enough to go on the
Super-Duper Loopy Loopy ride."

I say,
"There are still loads of
fun rides at the fair
for smaller people.

The **Chug-a-Bugs** ride
        is really exciting."

And Lola says,
"I don't think so, Charlie."

Then Lola says,
    "I have a GOOD plan.
I am going to **think** myself **bigger.**

Now I am **thinking** I am nearly
as **big** as a **sunflower**
touching the sun...

"And now I am thinking
            I am as **big** as one of those

extremely

TALLEST

buildings."

I say,
"You can't MAKE yourself **bigger**, Lola.
It just happens."

Lola says, "It's not fair. Why am I always, always the small one?"

So I say, "There are **great** things about being small. Like...

"... you get **stories** read
            to you every night...

and you get loads of **piggybacks**."

But Lola says,
    "I still really, **really** would
    like being the **biggest**."

When Marv comes over, he says,
"Are you ready for the
Super-Duper Loop the Looper?"

And Lola shouts,
"I am! I am! I am!"

Then Marv whispers,
"She's quite **small** for the ride,
isn't she, Charlie?"

And I say, "Yup."

"Aaagghh."

At the fair, Marv says,
  "The **Super-Duper Loop the Looper**
is going to be the best ride!"

"Yes. It will make our hair
  stand on end," I say.

"Ooohh!"

"And our tummies go all **funny**,"
                    says Marv.
        "I can't wait! How about you, Lola?"

"Err... I can't wait either..."

When we get to the front of the line,
Marv says,
"**Hold on** to your tummy, Lola!"

But Lola says,
"Err... I think I might be slightly too small still

Perhaps it would be
        a little more **fun** if I went on
something for more slightly
            smaller people – like the
Chug-a-Bugs!"

So we all go on the **Chug-a-Bugs**
and Lola **laughs** and **laughs**.

   She says, "You were right, Charlie!
The **Chug-a-Bugs** IS the very best ride
   in the whole world and the universe."